D1266715

Sommer-Time Stories—Classics

Sommer's lively retelling of this ancient oriental fable.

The Emperor and the Seed

Retold by Carl Sommer
Illustrated by Jorge Martinez

First Edition

Library of Congress Cataloging-in-Publication Data

Sommer, Carl, 1930-
The emperor and the seed / by Carl Sommer ; illustrated by Jorge Martinez. -- First edition.
pages cm. -- (Sommer-time stories-classics)
Summary: "In choosing a successor, the emperor has given Ming a seed to cultivate, but it will not grow. To make matters worse, all six of the other candidates grow vibrant plants. Is there hope for Ming? This story highlights the importance of honesty, even when it is difficult"-- Provided by publisher.
ISBN 978-1-57537-928-9 (library binding : alk. paper) -- ISBN 978-1-57537-934-0 (pdf) -- ISBN 978-1-57537-946-3 (kf8) -- ISBN 978-1-57537-940-1 (epub) [1. Folklore--China.] I. Martinez, Jorge, 1951- illustrator. II. Title.
PZ8.1.S6654Em 2016
398.2--dc23
[E]

2015007116

Once there was an emperor who ruled a great kingdom. One day he said to his wife, "We are getting old, and we do not have a son to become the next emperor. What should we do?"

"Why don't you ask your trusted advisors?" suggested the queen.

"Excellent!" exclaimed the emperor.

The emperor called his seven most trusted advisors. When the advisors came, they bowed before him and asked, "How may we serve you?"

"As you know," the emperor said, "I have no son. I have called you to advise me on the best

way to choose a ruler for our kingdom after I am gone."

The advisors offered suggestions. "Choose your nearest relative to become the next emperor," said one. "Choose the son of the richest man," said another.

"The general of your army has a son," said a third advisor. "Pick him to be the next emperor."

When the others were finished, Sun Han, the oldest advisor spoke, "For our kingdom to prosper, we need an emperor who is wise, courageous, and honest."

"I agree," said the emperor. "Just because a man is a relative or wealthy or the general's son,

does not mean he is courageous and a lover of truth and wisdom. But how can we find such a young boy whom we can train as the kingdom's future emperor?"

"Your Majesty," said Sun Han, "I suggest the advisors get seven of the best students in the kingdom and give them a test."

"What kind of test?" asked the emperor.

“It is a test that no one will know, but you, the emperor,” said Sun Han.

“Come and tell me,” said the emperor.

Sun Han went before the emperor and whispered into his ear what he should do. “Excellent!” exclaimed the emperor. “This test will show who is courageous and a lover of truth and wisdom.”

Immediately, the emperor ordered his advisors, “Each of you is to go to the towns and villages that you rule and choose a bright, courageous student who loves truth and wisdom. I will give you one month to find such a lad.

“I will give a test to the boys you choose. Then I plan on picking one of them. He and his family will come to the palace, and the boy will be trained to become the next emperor.”

As the advisors left, one of them asked, “What did Sun Han tell the emperor?”

“I don’t know,” said one of the advisors, “but I’m wondering if this is the wisest way for our kingdom to pick an emperor.”

“I’m wondering, too,” replied another advisor, “but we need to do our best. The future of our kingdom depends on whom we choose.”

Each advisor took an assistant in his chariot and began searching their towns and villages for the brightest, most courageous student who was also a lover of truth and wisdom.

Word of the emperor's plan spread quickly throughout the kingdom. Everyone was excited and asked questions. A woman said to her neighbor, "I wonder what kind of test the emperor will give."

"I don't know," her neighbor said, "but one thing I do know, we have a very wise emperor. I'm

sure it will be an excellent test."

When the advisors had chosen the boys they felt would become a wise ruler, they placed the boys and their families in their chariots. The people cheered as they passed by on their way to the palace. Everyone was excited over who would be the next emperor.

When the seven young boys stood before the emperor, he said, "It is a great honor that you have been picked as the brightest in the land. My plan is for one of you to be trained to become the next emperor.

"For a kingdom to be successful, an emperor must not only be wise, but should also be courageous and

a lover of truth. I will give each of you a test.

"Since our people live off the land, farming is very important. An emperor must know about crops and soil. In my hand is a container with a seed. You *must* use this seed. I will examine the plants that you bring back. I plan on picking one of you as the next emperor."

Everyone was in shock. No one could understand how a seed could show who is courageous and a lover of truth and wisdom.

"Bring the containers with the seeds!" ordered the emperor.

When the containers were placed before the emperor, he said to the boys, "I want you to go

to the library and research the best way to grow the seed. Discover the best type of soil and the right amount of water the seed needs. In one year you will show me what you have done."

The seven boys bowed. "Yes, Your Majesty," they said. Then each boy picked a container with a seed.

News spread quickly of the emperor's test. Many questioned his wisdom. "Did you hear about the foolish test the emperor made to pick our next ruler?" a woman said to her neighbor.

"Yes, I have," he said. "At first I trusted the emperor. But when I heard about the seeds, now I think it's foolish."

When the boys returned to their homes, each hoped to become the next emperor. They went to the library and spent much time researching about the best soils and the right amount of water so their seed would become the greatest plant.

Ming, one of the boys, carefully planted the seed and watered it with the best water. Eagerly he watched for the plant to sprout. But nothing happened!

After two months, Ming heard that the other boys' seeds were growing. "This seed should have sprouted in one month," Ming said to his dad. "Maybe my soil is bad. I'm going back to the library

and do more research. I'll try another soil."

After another two months, the seed still did not sprout. "Dad," groaned Ming, "what can I do? My seed still isn't growing."

Dad felt sorry for Ming. "You have done lots of research and have carefully obeyed the emperor's command," Dad said. "You have done your best. There's not much else you can do."

Word spread that Ming's seed was not growing. When one of his friends looked at his pot, he asked, "Why don't you plant another seed? No one will ever know."

"I can't do that!" exclaimed Ming. "That would be cheating. The emperor warned us not to use another seed."

In Ming's school many of the students laughed at him and called him names for not planting another seed. "Why are you so foolish?" a boy yelled out. "The emperor would never know if you used another seed."

"It's not right," replied Ming. "I will not use another seed. That would be dishonest."

"Then be a fool!" yelled the boy. "But you can be sure of one thing. You'll *never* be the next emperor!"

Now Ming hated to go to school because of being teased. "What's wrong with me?" Ming asked his mother. "I can't make my seed grow."

"There's nothing wrong with you," Mom said. "You tried your best. That's all you can do."

"When the emperor calls us back to the palace," said Ming, "I'm not going! I'm a big, big

failure! I'm *not* bringing an empty pot!"

Dad put his arm around Ming and said, "You never have to be ashamed when you do what is right. I want you to go to the emperor with your empty pot."

"Okay," whispered Ming. "I'll bring my empty pot. But I know I'm a big, big failure."

Finally, the time came for the seven boys to stand before the emperor. Six boys came back with beautiful plants. They were proud of what they had done.

Ming, however, was deeply ashamed for being such a big failure. He quickly put his empty pot in the front and said, "I'm walking to the back of the room to hide."

When the emperor walked in and saw the seven pots, he knew one of the boys would become the next emperor. As he walked slowly looking at the plants, he said, “These plants are beautiful. You must have done lots of hard work to grow such plants.”

“Yes,” said the six boys smiling.

When the emperor came to Ming’s pot, he stopped and asked, “What happened here?”

With his head down, Ming walked slowly from the back of the room. When he came to the emperor, he picked up his pot, bowed, and with tears flowing said, "Your Majesty, I have tried my best to do what you told us. I went to the library and searched for the best soil to make your seed grow. I watered the soil when it needed water.

"But the seed would not grow. Many of my

friends made fun of me. I am so sorry for being such a big, big failure."

"Son, what is your name?" asked the emperor.

"My name is Ming."

"Men and women," the emperor proclaimed, "I am happy to say that I have found the next emperor." Then after a long pause, "It is Ming!"

Everyone was in shock, above all, Ming.

Then the emperor explained, "The seeds I gave to the boys had all been cooked. They could not grow. Only this courageous lad, in spite of being made fun of by his friends, refused to cheat and plant another seed. Ming, you have shown that you

love truth, and you are courageous and honest. I ask you and your family to come to the throne."

Everyone clapped, except the six boys. They hung their heads in shame as Ming and his family walked to the throne.

Now people everywhere praised the emperor for what he had done. Ming's family moved into the palace, and Ming received training from the best teachers in the kingdom.

When the emperor became old, they had a great celebration to make Ming the next ruler. Ming, true to his word, became a courageous and wise emperor. Everyone loved him, for they knew that he would always be honest and do what was best for the kingdom.